KATHY HENDERSON was a commissioning editor at Penguin Books and The Open University before helping Frances Lincoln to found their children's list. An award-winning author, her many successful children's books include *The Middle of the Night*, *A Year in the City* and *The Little Boat* (winner of the 1995 Kurt Maschler Award, shortlisted for the Smarties Award 1995 and Highly Commended for the Kate Greenaway Award). Among her books for Frances Lincoln are *The Baby's Book of Babies*, *15 ways to get dressed*, *15 ways to go to bed* (shortlisted for the 1986 Smarties Prize), and *The Bedtime Book*, with Penny Ives.

CHARLOTTE HARD studied drawing and design at Manchester Polytechnic. Since graduating, she has worked as a freelance illustrator, specialising in children's books. Her work has appeared frequently in Playdays, and in educational and poetry books for OUP, and titles in the *Amazing Worlds* series from Dorling Kindersley. Her previous books include *One Green Island*, *Save Brave Ted*, and *The Wonderful World of Cameron the Cat* (all Walker).

For everyone in the back seat,
especially Annie, Dan and
Charley, and for all those
behind the wheel —
safe journey! — K.H.
To Richard, Max and Molly — C.H.

Cars, Cars, Cars! copyright © Frances Lincoln Limited 1999
Text copyright © Kathy Henderson 1999
Illustrations copyright © Charlotte Hard 1999
The right of Charlotte Hard to be identified as the Illustrator
of this work has been asserted by her in accordance with
the Copyright, Designs and Patents Act, 1988.

First published in Great Britain in 1999 by
Frances Lincoln Limited, 4 Torriano Mews
Torriano Avenue, London NW5 2RZ

First paperback edition 2000

Publisher's Note: The style of the artwork in this book is not
strictly realistic, and the characters do not always conform to
conventional health and safety requirements.

We would like to thank Nissan Motor Manufacturers (UK)
in Sunderland for showing us their factory.

ISBN 0-7112-1265-1 hardback
ISBN 0-7112-1382-8 paperback

Hand-lettering by Ellie Healey

Printed in Hong Kong

9 8 7 6 5 4 3 2 1

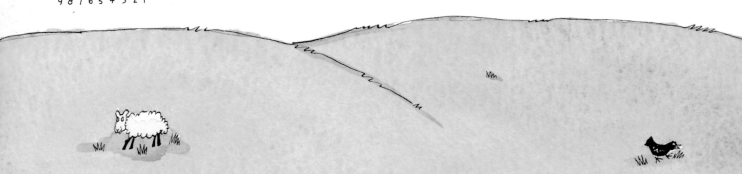

Cars, Cars, Cars!

Kathy Henderson

Illustrated by

Charlotte Hard

Frances Lincoln

se **robots** to **weld** them and paint them and bake them,

d the **seats** and the **engines**, the **wheels** and the tyres,

hile they're **moving** along on a **belt** in the air.

way to the **dealers** for someone to **buy** them.

Never mind. **Leave** it behind.
Just keep on going, you're bound to find
something **far** better-just follow the signs.

ROADS! ROADS! ROADS!

FASCINATING FACTS

★**Nobody knows** how many cars there are in the world. The best guess is over **540,000,000.** More than 37,000,000 **new cars** are **made** every year.

★That's **101,369** new cars **every day.** **4,224** new cars every hour of the day and night. **70 cars a minute!**

One motor car, two motor cars, three motor cars, four...

★If you put 540,000,000 motor cars **end to end**, they'd wrap right round the world **54** times!

Every year at **least** 470,000,000 new car **tyres** are made, and huge numbers of old ones are dumped, junked, buried, burnt...

The average family car belches out 200 kilograms of **pollutants** for every 1,000 kilometers it travels!

At least 3,500 people are **KILLED** in traffic accidents in the UK every year. In the USA, it's more than **40,000.** And if you survive that lot, by the time you're 80, you'll probably have spent **three years** of your life just **sitting** in a car.

MORE PICTURE BOOKS IN PAPERBACK FROM FRANCES LINCOLN

BUMPER TO BUMPER

Jakki Wood

Identify and learn the names of more than 30 vehicles, in the busiest, liveliest, most enormous traffic jam you've ever seen!

Suitable for National Curriculum — Nursery Level
Scottish Guidelines English Language — Nursery Level

ISBN 0-7112-1031-4   £4.99

BIG MACHINES

Angela Royston
Illustrated by Terry Pastor

An exciting introduction to big machines on the farm, on the road and around the building site.

Suitable for National Curriculum English — Reading, Key Stage 1
Scottish Guidelines English Language — Reading, Level A

ISBN 0-7112-0891-3   £4.99

THE PEBBLE IN MY POCKET

Meredith Hooper
Illustrated by Chris Coady

The story of the pebble reflects the history of our Earth with clear, dramatic text and vibrant illustrations.

Suitable for National Curriculum English — Reading, Key Stages 2 and 3; Science, Key Stages 2 and 3
Scottish Guidelines English Language — Reading, Level D; Environmental Studies — Level D

ISBN 0-7112-1076-4   £4.99

Frances Lincoln titles are available from all good bookshops. Prices are correct at time of publication, but may be subject to change.